This book
belongs to

_____

ON MY WAY WITH SESAME STREET™

Volume 14

In the Country

Featuring Jim Henson's Sesame Street Muppets

Children's Television Workshop/Funk & Wagnalls

Authors

Michaela Muntean
Rae Paige
Cathi Rosenberg-Turow
Norman Stiles

Illustrators

Tom Cooke
Tom Leigh
Joe Mathieu
Maggie Swanson

0-8343-0088-5

1 2 3 4 5 6 7 8 9 0

A Parents' Guide to
IN THE COUNTRY

This volume is chock-full of information about the natural environment. It introduces plants and animals. It explains how things grow and where food comes from. And it shows what it's like to live IN THE COUNTRY.

In "Big Bird's Day on the Farm," city slicker Big Bird finds out some fascinating facts. He discovers, for example, that milk comes from cows, not Hooper's Store.

In "Don't Worry, Snuffie," readers join Big Bird and Snuffie on their first camping trip.

"All Over Town" is an activity that depicts a typical country town. "Bert's Country Collections" presents the fascinating world of tiny creatures easily overlooked in the back yard. You can point them out in your own back yard or on a trip to the park.

Meanwhile, your children can enjoy their trip to the country with their Sesame Street friends.

The Editors
SESAME STREET BOOKS

Don't Worry, Snuffie

One hot summer day, a tall yellow bird named Big Bird and a big furry Snuffle-upagus named Snuffie climbed on to the Number 6 Sesame Street bus. Big Bird had a backpack on his back. It was stuffed with two sleeping bags, food, some pots and pans, and a few dishes. Snuffie was carrying a long pole wrapped with canvas. He held it tightly in his snuffle as he made his way to the back of the bus, saying "Excuse me," and "Pardon me." He was being very careful not to bump into anyone.

"We are going to have so much fun on our camping trip," Big
Bird said as they found seats on the bus. He unfolded a map
and spread it across his lap. "We are here. The Lazy Days
Campground is here. All we have to do is stay on this bus until
we get there. We can't miss it!"

Snuffie looked at the map. "It looks easy enough," he said.

"Of course it is," Big Bird answered. "Don't worry, Snuffie."

"Where will we sleep, Bird?" Snuffie asked.

"We are going to sleep in our tent," Big Bird said.

"Outside?" Snuffie asked.

"Of course," Big Bird said. "You can't put a tent up *inside*.
Sometimes you are a very silly Snuffle-upagus."

But Snuffie did not feel silly. He felt worried. He had never
been camping before. He had never slept outside before.

It was a long ride to the campground, and Snuffie was worried about missing their stop.

"Bird," he said finally, "we're here!"

Big Bird and Snuffie stepped off the bus and looked around. Big Bird took a deep breath of fresh country air. "Isn't this great?" he asked. "I told you not to worry, Snuffie."

Big Bird led the way as they walked to the campground office. The director said her name was Joan, and she showed them to their campsite.

"If you need any help," she said, "just ask." Then she told them where they could go swimming in the lake.

"There is a lifeguard on duty there," Joan explained. "Just follow the path with the orange signs."

Snuffie and Big Bird waved good-by to Joan.

"Now all we have to do is set up camp," said Big Bird.
"Do you know how to put up the tent?" Snuffie asked.
"Don't worry, Snuffie," said Big Bird. "It's easy. Just watch me."
Snuffie watched. He tried not to laugh when Big Bird got one side of the tent up, and the other side fell down. He tried hard not to laugh when Big Bird got tangled up in the canvas and fell down.

"Why don't I hold the middle pole with my snuffle while you tie the sides down," Snuffie finally suggested.
"Thanks, Snuffie," said Big Bird. "Let's cooperate."
Soon the tent was up and they had unrolled their sleeping bags. Snuffie looked around. The tent was like a little house, he thought. But he wondered what it would be like to sleep in the tent when it was dark outside.
"See?" said Big Bird. "I told you not to worry, Snuffie. It's not hard to put up a tent."

"Now let's go find that place to swim!" said Big Bird.

"Okay," said Snuffie, and he followed Big Bird down the path to the lake.

"Let's just walk across these stones," Big Bird said.

"Gee, Bird," Snuffie said. "They look awfully slippery. Why don't we stay on the path with the orange signs like Joan told us to?"

"Don't worry, Snuffie," Big Bird said. "This is a short cut. Watch me!"

Snuffie watched as Big Bird stepped on the first stone. SPLASH! He fell into the water.

"Quick!" Snuffie cried. "Grab onto my snuffle and I'll pull you out."

In a Snuffle-upagus second, Big Bird was out of the water and on dry land again.

"I think we'd better stay on the path this time," Big Bird said. "Then you won't be worried, Snuffie."

Soon they came to a lovely, sandy clearing beside the lake.
They waved to the lifeguard, and the lifeguard waved back.
All afternoon they swam and splashed in the lake. Snuffie used
his snuffle to spray water over his back. Then he used his snuffle
to squirt Big Bird.

"Wasn't it a great idea to go camping?" Big Bird said as they headed back to their campsite.

Snuffie agreed that it was a good idea. In fact, he had so much fun swimming that he had forgotten to worry about sleeping in the tent. But when they reached the campsite, he began to worry again.

"I brought hot dogs and marshmallows to roast over our camp fire," said Big Bird.

"Bird," said Snuffie, "do you know how to build a camp fire?"

"Don't worry, Snuffie," Big Bird said. "It's easy! All I have to do is rub two sticks together. Watch me!"

Snuffie watched as Big Bird found two sticks and began to rub them together. He rubbed and rubbed, but nothing happened.

"Gee," he said. "It always works on television."

Snuffie shuffled off toward the campground office.

"I'll be right back, Bird," he called over his shoulder.

Soon Snuffie returned with Joan. She showed them how to dig a deep pit, and then she started the fire.

"You should always have a grown-up help you build a fire and stay with you as long as the fire is burning," she told Big Bird and Snuffie.

They asked Joan to stay for dinner. She showed them how to roast hot dogs and marshmallows on long sticks over the coals. After dinner they sang songs around the camp fire. Joan told Big Bird and Snuffie about the forest paths they could explore the next day.

Then they looked up in the sky and wished on a star. Joan showed them how to find the Big and Little Dippers.

"It's time for me to go back," Joan said. So she showed Big Bird and Snuffie how to put out the fire. They helped her shovel dirt into the pit to make sure the fire was out.

As it got darker and darker, Snuffie got more and more worried. He wished he was back on Sesame Street in his own Snuffle-upagus bed.

"What a great day," Big Bird said as he crawled into his sleeping bag. "I'm exhausted."

Snuffie crawled into his sleeping bag, too. He was surprised by how soft and warm it felt. He snuggled down deep inside it. He lay there very quietly and tried hard not to worry.

Snuffie could hear the gentle rustling of the leaves in the forest. He could hear the sound of a bird in a tree. He began to think about that bird in its nest.

"That bird is camping out, too," he thought. "It is safe and warm in its nest, just like I am safe and warm inside my sleeping bag."

Snuffie began to think about all the other forest animals who were getting ready for bed. He thought about them so hard that he forgot about worrying.

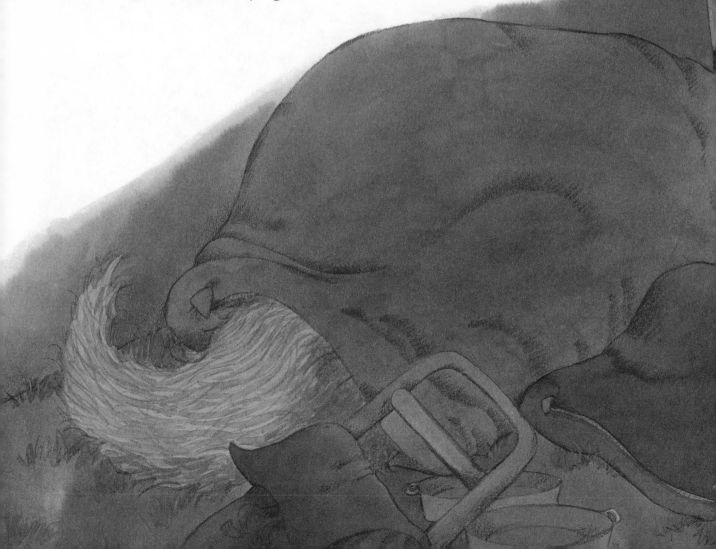

"Good night, Bird," Snuffie said.

"Good night, Snuffie," Big Bird answered.

But a few minutes later, Big Bird was still wide awake.

"Snuffie?" he said.

"Yes, Bird?" Snuffie asked sleepily.

"I can't go to sleep. It's too quiet here. I miss the sounds of the buses and cars and garbage trucks on Sesame Street. I miss my nest. I miss..."

"Isn't your sleeping bag soft and warm?" Snuffie asked.

"Yes," said Big Bird.

"Good. Snuggle down deep inside it," Snuffie said, and Big Bird did. "Now listen," said Snuffie. "Listen carefully. Do you hear the sound of that bird? She's saying, 'Cheep, cheep, go to sleep,' to her baby birds."

Big Bird listened. He could hear the chirping sound of a bird in the forest.

"Do you know that there are rabbits putting their baby bunnies to bed in rabbit holes all over the forest? There are mommy and daddy squirrels tucking their little squirrels into their beds in their tree homes."

"There are?" asked Big Bird.

"Oh, yes, Bird," Snuffie said. "There are all kinds of wonderful sounds in the forest, and all kinds of very sleepy babies. Bees are telling baby bees to stop their buzzing and shut their eyes. Little snakes are being told to stop hissing and to hush. Even the baby fish stop swimming and splashing as they get ready to go to sleep."

Thinking about all those sleepy babies in their forest homes made Big Bird very sleepy, too.

"Don't worry, Snuffie," Big Bird said dreamily. "I'll be able to go to sleep now."

"Sweet dreams, Bird," said Snuffie.

Bert's Country Collections

There are many little plants and insects you might not notice unless you look very carefully. Help Bert find these things.

After the Rain

Sometimes after the rain there is a rainbow in the sky. The colors in the rainbow are red, orange, yellow, green, blue, indigo, and violet.

Find each color in the rainbow.
Then find something
of each color in
the picture.

All Over Town

Sherlock Hemlock, the world's greatest detective, is looking all over town for Barkley the dog. Can you find Barkley?

hospital

general store

dry cleaner

shoe store

FIVE AND DIME

church

cemetery

gas station

GAS

restaurant

office building

bakery

paw prints

bank

BUS DEPOT

ice-cream parlor

drugstore

barbershop

BANK

LOADING ZONE

bus

florist

hardware store

police
station

synagogue

school

playground

library

post office

UNITED STATES POST OFFICE

paw prints

statue

Town
Hall

fire station

bookstore

paw prints

ENGINE COMPANY NO. 177

TOM'S BOOKS

Main Street

GROVER'S
Little Red Riding Hood

Trees

Greetings! If you count the rings in a tree trunk you can tell the age of the tree. There's one ring for each year. Let's count. One ring, two rings, three rings, four… This tree is four rings, I mean four years, old!

leaves

branches

trunk

roots

Leaves come in all different shapes and sizes, just as trees do.

This is my leaf collection. Can you make one, too? How many different kinds of leaves can you find where you live?

palm

maple

gingko

oak

mimosa

Flowers

My mommy will love these beautiful and adorable flowers.

How does your garden grow?
The soil of the earth, heat from the sun, and rain from the sky make plants and flowers grow.

rose

There are many, many different kinds of flowers. They grow almost everywhere on earth. Some flowers have a sweet smell.

daisy

carnation

lily

pansy

Do Cookies Grow on Trees?

Where does milk come from?
Cows. Mother cows make milk
in their bodies. Farmers milk the cows
and send the milk to a dairy
where it is put into bottles or cartons.

Where does butter come from?
Milk. Grover's great-grandmother used to make
butter in a wooden churn. Now machines do it.

Where does honey come from?
Bees make it from flower nectar, a sweet juice
in flowers. They store it in honeycomb, which is
made out of beeswax.

Where does chocolate come from?
Beans that grow on a tree called the cacao tree.

Where do eggs come from?
Chickens lay eggs.

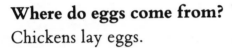

Where does vanilla come from?
Vanilla beans, which grow on a climbing orchid plant.

Hmmm. Milk...butter... honey...chocolate...eggs... vanilla...flour. That's where COOOOKIES come from!

Farmer Grover's Farm

Farmer Grover's friends are helping him do the chores. What is everybody doing?

chimney

weather vane

farmhouse

pulley

hay bales

hayloft

stalls

silo

barn

cow

hose

dog

pitchfork

bucket

goat

horse

colt

pail

pig

piglets

duck

ducklings

pigpen

duck pond

Big Bird's Day on the Farm

Big Bird was on his way to Sesame Street when he saw a sign at a fork in the road. It said, "No Through Road."

"What a funny name for a road," said Big Bird. "Maybe this is the way to Sesame Street," he said as he walked along the dirt road.

"Hi there!" Big Bird greeted a flock of chickens pecking on the road. "Do you mind if I join you for dinner?" Then he looked up and saw a little girl.

"You're the biggest chicken I've ever seen," she said.

"I'm not a big chicken. I'm Big Bird," he said.

"Nice to meet you, Big Bird. I'm Ruthie, and this is my brother Floyd."

"Would you like to visit our farm, Big Bird?" asked Ruthie.

"Oh, thanks," he answered. "It's too late for me to get all the way to Sesame Street today."

Ruthie and Floyd took Big Bird to the barn. They made him a soft nest out of hay. "Will you stay and play with us tomorrow?" Floyd asked.

"I'd like that," Big Bird answered.

"When the rooster crows, you'll know it's time to get up," said Ruthie.

Big Bird waited and waited for the rooster to crow. "Maybe he's taking a nap," Big Bird thought as he fell asleep.

"Cockadoodledooooo!" Big Bird woke up and saw the sun coming up.

After breakfast Ruthie and Floyd took Big Bird to help them milk the cows.

"Gee!" said Big Bird. "On Sesame Street we get our milk from Hooper's Store."

Next they went to the henhouse. Ruthie and Floyd showed Big Bird how to take eggs out of the nests gently and carry them carefully in an egg basket.

"Gee," said Big Bird. "On Sesame Street we get our eggs in cartons."

Then Ruthie and Floyd took Big Bird to the pigpen to feed the pigs.

When they went out to the field to feed the horses, Big Bird carried the bag of oats. They poured the oats into troughs for the horses.

"Bert likes oatmeal, too," said Big Bird. "He would love it here!"

"Now we'll show you where honey comes from," said Ruthie, leading Big Bird out in the field to the beehives. "The bees gather nectar from the flowers, and they bring it here to their hive. Then they turn it into honey."

"Don't pet the bees," said Floyd.

Then Big Bird, Ruthie, and Floyd went to the apple orchard. "I know how to pick these apples fast," said Big Bird. Without even standing on tiptoe, Big Bird could reach every apple on the tree.

In the garden Ruthie and Floyd picked carrots and tomatoes. Big Bird couldn't believe it. "Gee," he said. "On Sesame Street we get our vegetables from Mr. McIntosh's fruit-and-vegetable stand."

Now the sun was high in the sky. They went to the house for a delicious farm lunch. Then it was time for Big Bird to go home.

"Come and visit us again," said Ruthie and Floyd.

"Thanks for everything," said Big Bird. "I had a wonderful day on the farm. By the way, can you tell me how to get to Sesame Street?"

Starry Night

A summer night,
The stars are bright.
Monsters are dancing
In the moonlight.

There is only one moon, but there are many stars.
Count the stars in the sky. How many can you see? $\dfrac{20}{4}$

Count the monsters. How many are there?